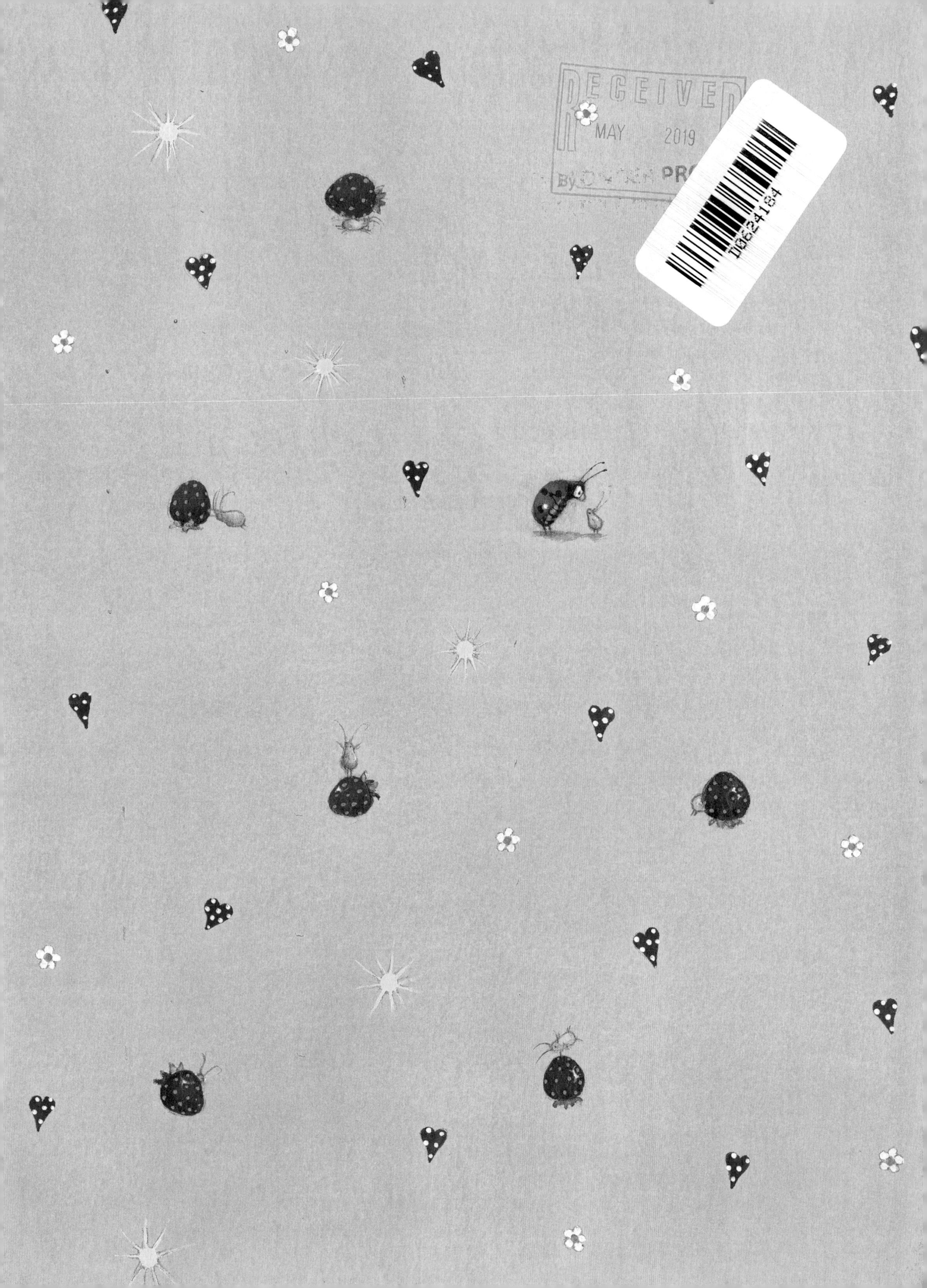

The illustrations in this book are hand-drawn using pencils, watercolour paint, pastels and gouache.

Translated by Polly Lawson. First published in German as *Erdbeerinchen Erdbeerfee Alles voller Sonnenschien*
by Arena Verlag GmBH 2013. First published in English by Floris Books in 2019

British Library CIP data available ISBN 978-178250-560-0
Printed in China through Asia Pacific Offset Ltd

Evie and the Strawberry Patch Rescue

Stefanie Dahle

“I love it when it rains!” giggled Evie the Strawberry Fairy. Heavy raindrops were falling and making deep puddles. Evie jumped up and down in her garden, splashing in the puddles and squelching mud between her bare toes.

I ♥ my garden
COMPOST

But a week later it was *still* raining non-stop. Evie's house was flooded, and her strawberry patch was swamped. She wasn't enjoying splashing around any more. Now her soaking-wet feet were freezing cold.

"Achoo!" she sneezed. "I've got a runny nose. Achoo!"

Just then, a huge rush of water shot down the spout of Evie's teapot home and drenched her from the curls of her hair to the tips of her toes.

"I can't stand it any more, and neither can my strawberry patch!" cried Evie to her best friend Brightwing Butterfly. "The berries will rot if they sit in puddles."

Brightwing Butterfly suggested making a big umbrella.

Briar the Blackberry Fairy found a huge rhubarb leaf. A strong beetle helped Brightwing hold it over the berries, but the rain kept falling and the flood rose higher.

"It's no use." Evie sighed. "I have to rescue my poor strawberries! It's time to find somewhere else to live until this flood dries up."

First, Evie asked at the fairy tree, where lots of her fairy friends lived.

"Hello!" she called. "My house and my strawberry patch are flooded! Do you have any room for us?"

Skye the Air Fairy said, "I'm so sorry, Evie, but the fairy tree is full right now."

Next, Evie looked around the pond, but it was too swampy. "These buttercups love the water, but my strawberries won't. This is just as wet as my teapot house!"

Then she explored the berry wood, but it was too dark. "My strawberries will need lots of sunlight to grow!"

At last, high on a hill, Evie found an old birdhouse that had fallen from a tree.

"Perfect!" she cried. "With a little work, this could be a cosy cottage. My strawberries will be safe from floods and get plenty of sunlight up here too."

Evie's friends helped to pack up her belongings. Darcy the Dandelion Fairy and Brightwing Butterfly did their best to dry everything out.

Evie was worried about how to move her strawberries.

"We need someone strong to dig up the plants and carry them," said Brightwing Butterfly.

"What about the squirrel?" suggested Darcy.

"Of course!" cried Evie in delight. "I always give her some strawberry jam in winter. I'm sure she'll help!"

The squirrel gladly agreed, and she even brought extra helpers with her! A toad and two voles carefully dug up the tender roots and the squirrel carried the strawberry plants to a cart pulled by a hedgehog.

Soon they were ready to go and Evie said goodbye to her flooded home. "Bye bye, teapot house! We'll be back when you've dried out!"

Evie loved the birdhouse and soon settled in happily.
But her strawberry plants looked pale and weak.
Extra compost didn't help.

"What's wrong?" asked Evie. "Why aren't you growing?"
She peered under their leaves to check their roots...

...and found lots of greenfly munching on the berries!

"You cheeky little things!" scolded Evie. But the greenfly just giggled and kept on nibbling.

"The ladybugs usually chase away the greenfly," said Brightwing Butterfly. "Where are they?"

Evie's eyes opened wide. "Oh no!" she cried. "I forgot to ask them to come with us!"

She grabbed a basket and rushed off.

Back at her old flooded house,
Evie found the ladybugs. "I'm sorry we left you behind, dear bugs," she said. "Would you like to see my new strawberry patch? It's dry, and there are lots of greenfly to chase!"

The ladybugs eagerly hopped into her basket. Evie grasped the handle, and at that moment a friendly bat flew down.

"Hello Evie," he said. "Would you like to ride on my back and I'll carry your basket?"

"Yes please!" cried Evie, and they soared off in the starlight.

The next morning, Evie showed the ladybugs her new strawberry patch. As soon as the greenfly saw the bugs coming, they stopped giggling and scuttled away!

“The strawberries look better already,” said Evie. “Well done, ladybugs!”

To say thank you, she built the bugs a house to live in. She filled it with old sticks and damp leaves, and stuffed the roof with straw to make it cosy.

I ♥ my garden

"Ah," said Evie. "It's lovely to be warm and dry again. And look! My strawberries are so red and juicy!"

"It's a shame you had to leave the teapot," said Brightwing Butterfly, "but the birdhouse is a lovely place to stay for a while. Home sweet home!"

"As sweet as my strawberries," giggled Evie.

Evie stretched out happily in her garden, enjoying the sweet smell of strawberries and the warm sunshine on her bare toes.

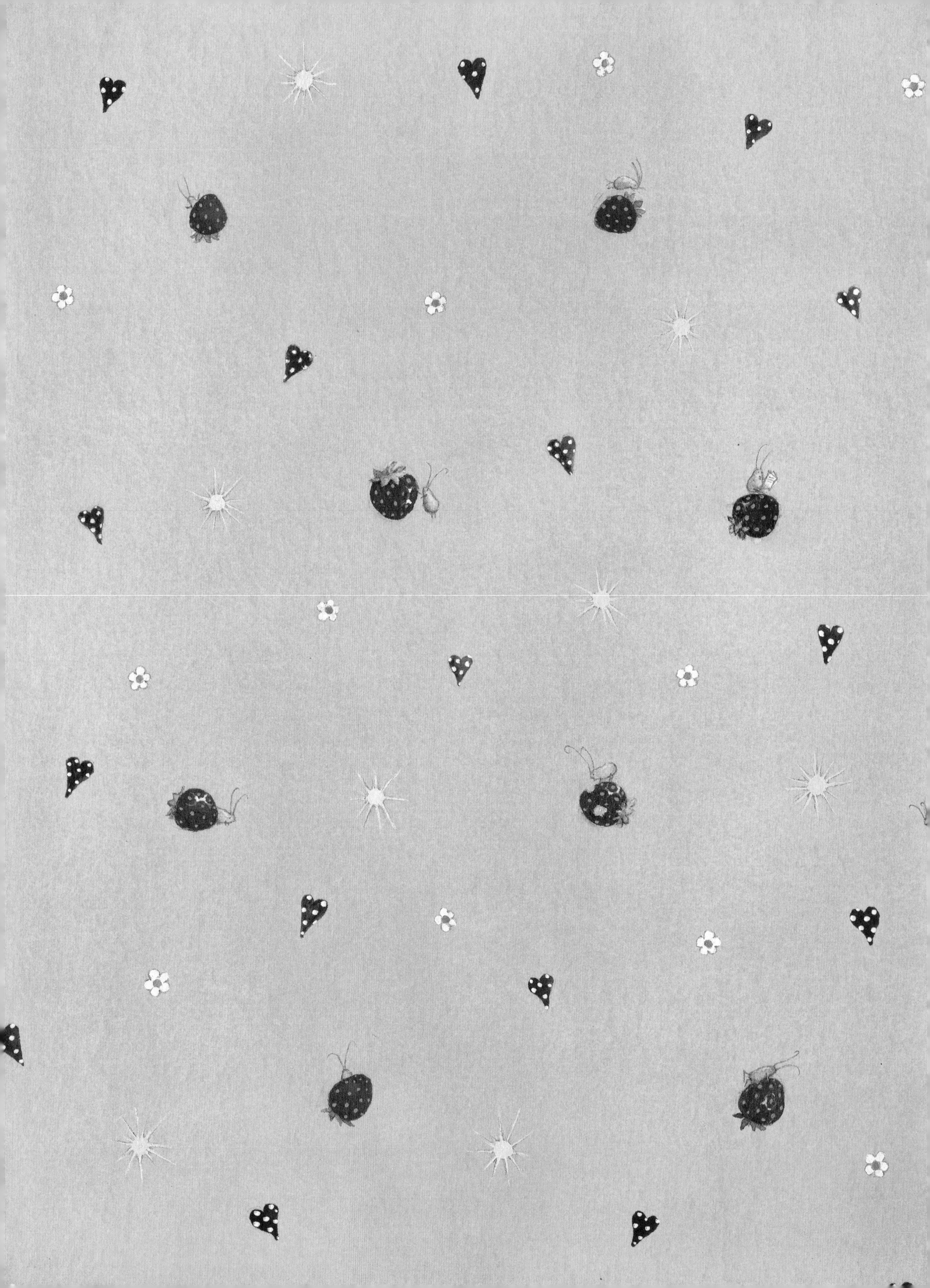